For the Barry
who is not a fish

SIMON & SCHUSTER
This edition first published 2009
by Simon & Schuster UK Ltd
1st Floor, 222 Gray's Inn Road, London, WC1X 8HB
A CBS Company

A CIP catalogue record for this book is available
from the British Library upon request

ISBN: 978 1 4711 7727 9
ISBN: 978 0 85707 397 6 (eBook)

Printed in China

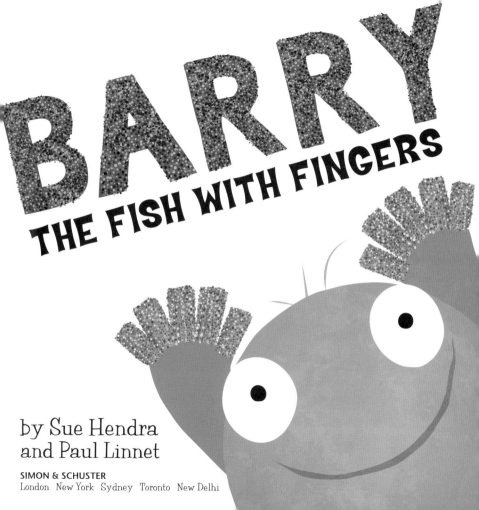

BARRY
THE FISH WITH FINGERS

by Sue Hendra
and Paul Linnet

SIMON & SCHUSTER
London New York Sydney Toronto New Delhi

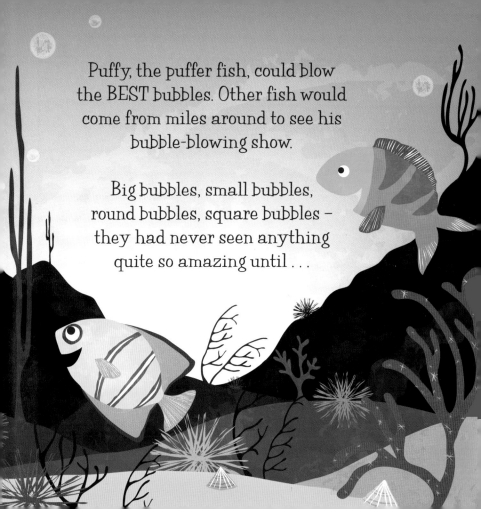

Puffy, the puffer fish, could blow
the BEST bubbles. Other fish would
come from miles around to see his
bubble-blowing show.

Big bubbles, small bubbles,
round bubbles, square bubbles –
they had never seen anything
quite so amazing until . . .

They caught sight of Barry.

Barry was no ordinary fish.

Barry was a fish with **fingers!**

Suddenly, everyone wanted to find out more about the amazing fish with fingers.

"What can your fingers do, Barry?" they asked. "Tell us, tell us!"

"Well," said Barry. "Fingers mean . . ."

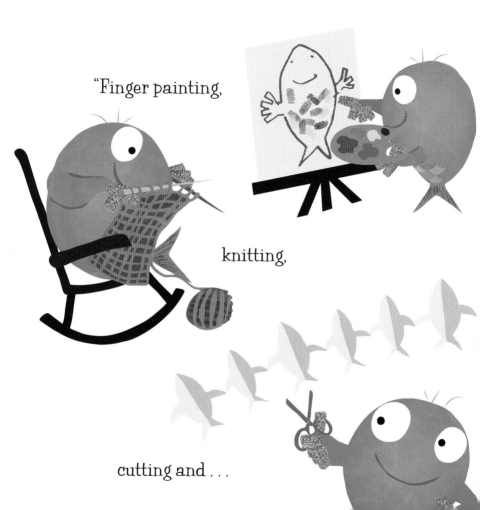

"Finger painting,

knitting,

cutting and . . .

FINGER PUPPETS!

But, best of all,
fingers mean ..."

The fish had never had so much fun.
"Come on, Puffy. Join in!" said Barry.

But Puffy didn't want to join in.
He was feeling sad.

"Now nobody wants to see my bubble-blowing show,"
he sighed. "I hate Barry's fingers. They're stupid!"

So while Puffy sulked on his own, Barry and the other fish had a whale of a time, chasing each other through sea caves, in and out of seashells and through the seaweed.

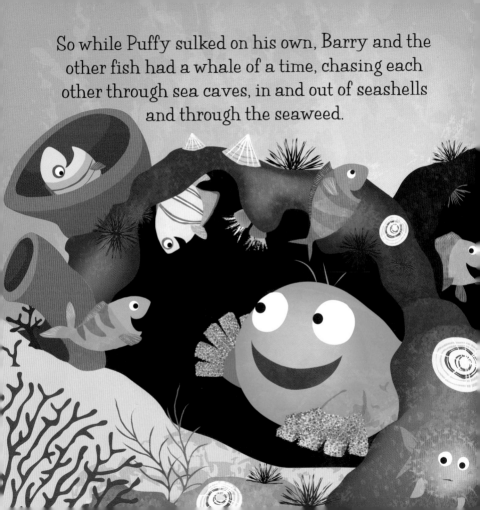

But, all of a sudden, Barry stopped dead in his tracks.

He heard a loud splash and a rumbling noise.

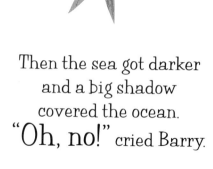

Then the sea got darker and a big shadow covered the ocean. "Oh, no!" cried Barry.

"Oh, no!" cried the fish.
A huge crate had fallen into the water
and it was going to squash Puffy.

And that was when Barry did something truly amazing –

he pointed!
"Look out, Puffy!"

RAGILE
HANDLE WITH CARE
Musical Instruments
For: Mr Drum,
Guitar Lane,
Songville,
Tune Town.

Was it too late?
Had poor Puffy been squashed?

Phew!
No, he hadn't.

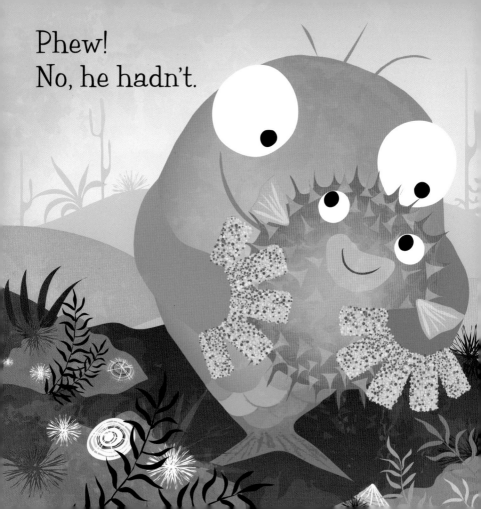

"Thank you, Barry," said Puffy. "You saved
my life. I'm sorry for being a grumpy spoilsport.
Can we play tickle chase?"

But Barry had a better idea . . .

"LET'S PARTY!"

"Take it away, Puffy!" he cried.
So Barry played the piano, Puffy blew the trumpet
and everyone had the BEST time ever.